The Long Dog

by Eric Seltzer

SCHOLASTIC INC.

For Maia and Josie —E.S.

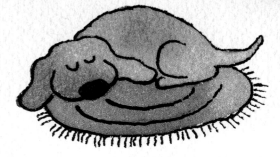

Copyright © 2015 by Eric Seltzer

All rights reserved. Published by Scholastic Inc., *Publishers since 1920.* SCHOLASTIC and associated logos are trademarks and/or registered trademarks of Scholastic Inc.

The publisher does not have any control over and does not assume any responsibility for author or third-party websites or their content.

No part of this publication may be reproduced, stored in a retrieval system, or transmitted in any form or by any means, electronic, mechanical, photocopying, recording, or otherwise, without written permission of the publisher. For information regarding permission, write to Scholastic Inc., Attention: Permissions Department, 557 Broadway, New York, NY 10012.

This book is a work of fiction. Names, characters, places, and incidents are either the product of the author's imagination or are used fictitiously, and any resemblance to actual persons, living or dead, business establishments, events, or locales is entirely coincidental.

ISBN 978-0-545-74632-8

10 9 8 7 6 5 4 3 2 1   15 16 17 18 19/0

Printed in the U.S.A.   40
First printing, August 2015
Book design by Maria Mercado

CALLING ALL DOGS!

This is a hot dog.

This is a cold dog.

This is a
young dog.

This is an
old dog.

And here comes
a long dog.

This is a day dog.

This is a night dog.

This is a
black dog.

This is a
white dog.

And this is that long dog.

This is a high dog.

This is a low dog.

This is a
fast dog.

This is a
slow dog.

This is still one long dog.

This is a wet dog.

This is a dry dog.

This is a gal dog.

This is a guy dog.

How long is this dog?

This is a king dog.

This is a queen dog.

This is a dirty dog.

This is a clean dog.

This is a
nice dog.

This is a
mean dog.

And there goes that long dog.

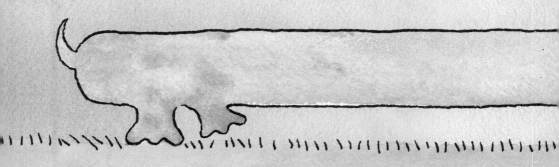

Can you say so long, dogs?